# THIS BOOK BELONGS TO:

_____

# IN
# MS. MCFADDEN'S
# CLASS

By
## SUEWONG D. MCFADDEN
Illustrated by
## KAYLA HARGROVE

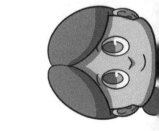

# DEDICATION

To Bethesda Elementary, who gave me the opportunity to grow as an educator.

To my first—year students," My Little Emojis," who have made my first year of teaching an unforgettable experience.

To the Singletary Family, who I dedicate this book to Zaiden Singletary. You all have made such an impact on my life. I am so blessed to embark on this new journey with you all right beside me.

# HEY, I AM ZAY, THAT IS WHAT MY FRIENDS CALL ME.

# MY FAMILY CALLS ME ZAI-SWAY BECAUSE I AM WAY TOO COOL!

I AM IN SECOND-GRADE AND I REALLY DON'T LIKE IT. IT IS SUPER, SUPER, SUPER BORING. I DON'T LIKE TO READ, I DON'T LIKE TO WRITE, AND I REALLY DON'T LIKE MATH.

IT IS NOT LIKE FIRST GRADE WITH MS. MCFADDEN.
SHE IS THE BEST TEACHER IN THE WHOLE-WIDE WORLD!
SHE IS THE BEST TEACHER IN THE UNIVERSE!
SHE IS THE BEST TEACHER OF ALL TIME!

IN MS. MCFADDEN'S CLASS, WE GOT TO READ BOOKS WITH BOOK BUDDIES.

WE ALWAYS FOUGHT OVER THE TURTLE PILLOWS.

I ALWAYS WON!

# IN MS. MCFADDEN'S CLASS, SHE LETS US PLAY AROUND ON THE MAGIC BOARD USING THE MAGIC PENS!

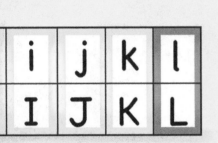

i j k l
I J K L

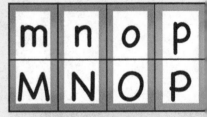

m n o p
M N O P

IN MS. MCFADDEN'S CLASS,
SHE TOLD US
SILLY STORIES
ABOUT HOW SHE WAS
A PRINCESS
WHO TRAVELED AROUND
THE WORLD.

I DIDN'T BELIEVE HER ... AT FIRST.

IN MS. MCFADDEN'S LESSON, WE PLAYED A GROUP GAME USING BUZZERS! MS. MCFADDEN ALWAYS TRIED TO BEAT US, BUT TABLE 4 STILL WON!

IN MS. MCFADDEN'S CLASS, WE HAD A HUGE CELEBRATION WITH BALLOONS, GIFTS, AND FOOD!

WE ALSO GOT MATCHING T-SHIRTS!

IN MR. NEWSON'S CLASS,
I WONDERED IF WE WERE
HAVING A PARTY.
I CHECKED UNDERNEATH
THE TABLE FOR GIFTS. I LOOKED
IN THE CLOSET
FOR BALLOONS.
I EVEN ASK ONE OF MY FRIENDS
IF WE WERE HAVING A PARTY.

HMM...I WONDER...

"NOPE, NOT HERE!"

"NO BALLOONS IN HERE!"

"DID YOU HEAR ANYTHING?"

THIS IS WHY
I HAVE TO GO BACK TO
FIRST GRADE
BECAUSE I NEED
MS. MCFADDEN
TO TEACH ME
ALL OVER
AGAIN.

NOW, SHE HAS NEW STUDENTS THIS YEAR, AND I AM SO J-E-A-L-U-S. I WILL NOT TELL HER THAT BECAUSE I AM A BOY AND BOYS DON'T SHARE THEIR FEELINGS!

"ZAY, I HEARD YOU WERE HAVING SOME TROUBLE MOVING ON FROM FIRST GRADE, BUT WE DID HAVE AN AWESOME YEAR, DIDN'T WE?" MS. MCFADDEN BRAGGED.

"YEAH, WE DID!" I SAID.

"NO ONE SAID, GROWING UP WAS GOING TO BE EASY. IT IS GOING TO TAKE SOME TIME.

I HAVE TAUGHT YOU EVERYTHING YOU NEEDED TO KNOW, SO YOU CAN BE THE BEST THAT YOU CAN BE.

YOU HAVE GROWN SO MUCH THIS YEAR, AND THERE IS SO MUCH MORE YOU NEED TO LEARN..."

"...SO, YOU HAVE TO GIVE SECOND-GRADE
AND MR. NEWSON A TRY.

WE ARE ALL ROOTING FOR YOU!
SO, SHOW OUT A LITTLE AND GIVE US ALL
YOU GOT!"

"I WILL TRY." I TOLD HER.

"GUESS WHAT ELSE, ZAY! NO MATTER WHAT
I WILL ALWAYS BE THERE FOR YOU.
I PROMISE." SHE WHISPERED.

I SMILED, BUT NOT TOO MUCH
BECAUSE I AM A BOY, AND
BOYS DON'T SHARE THEIR FEELINGS!

AFTER A WHILE, SECOND-GRADE WAS NOT SO BAD, AND I WORK VERY HARD. MR. NEWSON WAS VERY PROUD OF ME!

# ABOUT THE AUTHOR

Suewong McFadden was born in the Bronx of New York City, but raised in Lexington, North Carolina, alongside her mother and siblings. In 2009, she graduated from Lexington Senior High School. In 2016, she obtained her B.A in Theatre with a Minor in Education from the infamous HBCU, North Carolina Central University.

For three years, McFadden has been teaching First Grade at Bethesda Elementary. She is a member of various organizations such as Zeta Phi Beta Sorority, Incorporated, Golden Key International Honor Society, Phi Eta Sigma National Honor Society, Kappa Delta Pi International Honor Society in Education, and Phi Epsilon Chapter of Order of Omega. She has written several plays and screenplays. "In Ms. McFadden's Class" will be the first edition of the new Ms. McFadden's children book series.

She loves working with children and mentoring kids of all ages. She hopes to create many stories to impact families and children around the world.

CPSIA information can be obtained
at www.ICGtesting.com
Printed in the USA
LVHW011600290520
656908LV00005B/133